DINO RIDERS

How to Rope a Giganotosaurus

Don't miss:

How to Tame a Triceratops
How to Hog-Tie a T-Rex
How to Catch a Dino Thief

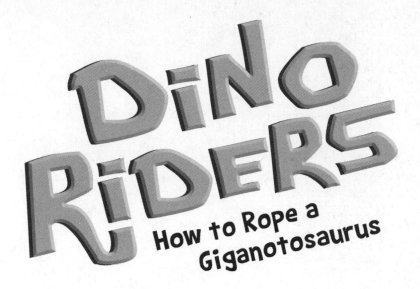

DINO RIDERS

How to Rope a Giganotosaurus

Will Dare

sourcebooks
jabberwocky

Published by Sourcebooks Jabberwocky, an imprint of Sourcebooks, Inc.
P.O. Box 4410, Naperville, Illinois 60567-4410
(630) 961-3900
Fax: (630) 961-2168
www.sourcebooks.com

Library of Congress Cataloging-in-Publication Data

Names: Dare, Will, author.
Title: How to rope a Giganotosaurus / Will Dare.
Description: Naperville, Illinos : Sourcebooks Jabberwocky, [2017] | Series:
    Dino riders ; 2 | Summary: After recording the facts in his Dino Cowboy
    Diary about the biggest dinosaur in existence, Josh brings his friends Sam
    and Abi along on his mission to capture one.
Identifiers: LCCN 2016016724 | (13 : alk. paper)
Subjects: | CYAC: Dinosaurs--Fiction.
Classification: LCC PZ7.1.D32 Hn 2016 | DDC [Fic]--dc23 LC record available
at https://lccn.loc.gov/2016016724

Printed and bound in the United States of America.
VP 10 9 8 7 6 5 4 3 2 1

With special thanks to Barry Hutchison.

CHAPTER

1

It was early evening, and the sun was beginning its slow creep down the sky. Josh Sanders and his friends, Sam and Abi, were moseying on into town. They had money in their pockets, errands to run, and several tons of dinosaur plodding along beneath them. It was just another day in Trihorn County, and Josh was hungry for adventure.

"Race you into town," he suggested. Charge,

his triceratops, gave an excited snort. It had only been a few weeks since Josh had ridden the 'cera in the Founders' Day race, and they'd both been itching for another dose of excitement ever since.

Abi and Sam looked down at their own dinosaurs. They each rode their own gallimimus—a long-necked dinosaur, which was capable of some impressive bursts of speed.

"Deal," said Abi.

"See you at the finish line," Sam laughed, then he and Abi kicked their heels, spurring their dinosaurs into action.

"Hey, wait, no fair!" Josh cried as his friends sped off toward Trihorn settlement. He leaned forward in the saddle and whispered into Charge's ear, "You ready, buddy?"

Charge snorted and nodded his enormous head. Josh patted him on one of his horns and then straightened up. "Let's at least give them a head start," he said, a sly grin creeping across his face. "Three…two…one…go!"

Josh gripped the reins as Charge shot forward, the dino's powerful feet thundering across the dry ground. Josh thought back to the frantic sprint to the finish line he and Charge had made in the Founders' Day race. He'd only owned Charge for a few days before the race, but that hadn't stopped Josh from riding to victory.

The world whistled by in a blur of brown and blue. Sam and Abi both turned in their saddles as Charge powered up behind them. They stood in their stirrups, flicking the reins as fast as they could, but no matter how fast their dinosaurs ran, they were no match for the triceratops.

"Last one to the store's a diplodocus dropping!" Josh grinned wildly, thundering past.

Charge raced along Main Street, dodging past a group of dinos tied to a tethering post outside the saloon, then slowing for a moment

as they passed the sheriff's office. The sheriff didn't much approve of dinosaurs running down Main Street. Then again, he didn't much approve of anything.

Charge gave a final burst of speed, then skidded to a halt outside the town store. He stopped so abruptly, his back legs lifted off the ground, and Josh had to grab on to the dino's armored

fringe to stop himself from being flung through the air.

Josh swung out of the saddle just as Sam and Abi trotted up. They and their dinosaurs were all breathing heavily, while Charge had barely broken a sweat.

"Argh, I miscalculated the turn trajectories!" Sam protested. "I'd have won if I hadn't done that."

Charge turned and loudly bottom-burped in Sam's direction. Josh pinched his nose and laughed. "I think Charge disagrees!"

Sam wrinkled his nose and jumped out of the way of the toxic gas.

"All righty then," said Abi. "What are we here for again?"

"My dad's errands," Josh said with a groan as he began to make his way toward the general store. "C'mon, let's get it over with…"

Suddenly though, he stopped as he spotted a large crowd gathered along the street. Molly, a girl from school, stood in the middle of the group, passing out copies of the *Daily Diplodocus* newspaper that were being eagerly snatched out of her hands.

"What's all the hubbub?" Abi asked, swinging down from her dino.

Josh shrugged. "Only one way to find out, I guess."

They made their way through the crowd, ducking under armpits and avoiding elbows. Josh stepped to the front just in time for Molly

to roar in his face. "Extra, extra, read all about it! Terrordactyl Bill does it again!"

Josh's eyes went wide. Terrordactyl Bill was his hero! He was the greatest, most fearless dino rider who had ever lived, and Josh dreamed of being just like him. When T-Bill had presented the prizes at the Founders' Day race, he'd given Josh his hat. When Josh wore it—which he always did—he could imagine T-Bill's dino-riding energy flowing right into him. (Either that or his dandruff. He was never quite sure.)

"What did he do this time?" Josh asked.

"Well, he only went and caught himself a T. rex!" Molly cried.

Josh gasped. "Whoa!"

"Ain't that an understatement?" Molly

nodded. "One of the biggest meat eaters that ever lived. One of the most fearsome too."

"And T-Bill caught one?" asked Josh breathlessly.

"Yessir. With his bare hands. In the middle of a tornado," said Molly. "While he was on fire," she added after a pause.

Abi peered over Josh's shoulder at the newspaper Molly was holding. "Where does it say he was on fire?" she asked.

"You calling me a liar?" Molly frowned. She pulled the newspaper away. "And no spyin' without buyin', so pay up or move along."

Josh fished in his pocket for a coin, but before he could find one, the town bell began to chime. "Five o'clock," Josh said with a gasp, spinning on the spot. His dad had sent him to the store on an errand, and the store was about to close. Dad wouldn't be pleased if Josh came home empty-handed, so, thrusting the coin into Molly's hand, he snatched up the paper and ducked back through the crowds.

Josh and his friends raced toward the general store and clattered through the door just before the store owner, Old Man Jones, could turn the "closed" sign around.

Old Man Jones had been ancient for as long as anyone could remember. He had a wispy white beard and a shiny, bald head. He walked with a stoop, and although he looked like a strong wind might snap him in half, Josh had seen him lifting boxes that men a quarter of his age would struggle to move.

"Well now, what have we here?" croaked Mr. Jones, squinting at the children.

"It's Josh Sanders, Mr. Jones. My dad said I have something to pick up."

The old man stroked his beard. "Did he now? You know, I think I do recall something…what was it?"

Josh, Sam, and Abi waited patiently while Mr. Jones tried to remember.

"What was it?" he muttered. "I swear, sometimes I think I'd forget my own…what d'you call it?" he said. "With the face on."

"Head?" suggested Sam.

Old Man Jones nodded. "That's it. Sometimes

I swear I'd forget my own head if it wasn't screwed on." He looked the children up and down. "Now then, what can I do for you?"

Josh shot the others a sideways glance, then tried again. "My dad said there's something I have to pick up."

Mr. Jones clapped his hands and raised his finger. "Yessir, that's right. I got it. Follow me," he said, beckoning them toward the back door.

Josh, Sam, and Abi stepped out into the backyard and gasped in horror at the stench. It was a rotten, sulfur-like smell that hit them like a head butt from an armor-headed pachycephalosaurus.

"Ew, what is that?" Abi asked as she wheezed, burying her nose in the crook of her arm.

"Cabbages!" announced Old Man Jones, holding up a bucket full of sloppy, decaying vegetables. "All rotted beautifully—just right for them iguanodons you got up at the ranch."

He thrust the bucket into Josh's hands. A big glug of the smelly glop sloshed all down his front and into his boots. Suddenly, Josh knew why his dad was so keen for *him* to do the errand.

"Grab a few and start loading up," Old Man Jones said. "You got lots to carry."

"How many?" asked Sam.

The shopkeeper pulled aside a sheet of sackcloth, revealing twenty or more buckets festering under a swarm of flies.

"That many," he said.

Josh groaned and squelched his way over to the buckets. Sam and Abi shot him icy glances as they began loading them up.

T-Bill gets to go out and have grand adventures, Josh thought. *And all I get is a cold shower of rotten cabbage. If only my life could be more like T-Bill's.*

And just like that, Josh had an idea...

T-BILL TRAPS T.REX!

Dino rider pummels predator

which the ... hero saves settlement cruely ... a rem ... that ... only 35 buildings trampled and destroyed! It ... one of the less

COMET CON!

... wever, most people ... top officals call for calm ... time of the incident ...

"No chance that space rock could hit Lost Plains," said the lead ...

... as likely as "man walking on moon."

... s an exciting day ...
Tyrannosaurs edge it in 24–20 win

In the se... of the game, the dino egg was mistaken for football, ... de for quite a surp...

TRIHORN TYRANNOSAURS
VS SCALY POINT SAUROPODS
MATCH REPORT

...at the referee was plucked from the ground by hungry pterodactyl. Witnesses said they saw a great

CHAPTER 2

The next morning, Josh jumped from his bed and reached under his pillow for his journal. He flipped through the pages, glancing through his scribbled notes, lengthy lists, and detailed dino drawings. Everything Josh knew about dinosaurs was in the notebook, and today, he was going to add to it.

Josh hurriedly pulled on his pants, shirt, and waistcoat, then slipped his feet into his iguanodon-hide boots. Unhooking his hat from the door, he plopped it on top of his head. His mom didn't approve of him wearing the hat at the breakfast table, but if his plan was going to work, he'd need all the T-Bill energy he could get.

Racing into the kitchen, Josh almost screamed as a chalk-white figure grabbed at him from behind the door. At first, he thought it was a ghost, but then he realized it was his mom, covered from head to toe in flour. Josh's stomach rumbled hungrily. A flour-covered

Mom at this time of day could mean only one thing: she'd been baking her legendary breakfast pie.

"What did I tell you about that hat?" Mom asked.

Josh smiled broadly. "Mornin'," he said. "I know, but I've got a real good reason for wearing it today."

Mom tapped her foot. "Which is?"

Josh's smile widened even further. "I can't say right now, but as soon as I can, you'll be the first to know."

He stretched up and kissed her on the cheek, then sat at the table and cut himself a chunk of breakfast pie.

"You're mighty bright and cheerful this

morning," Mom said. She wiped her hands on her apron and was almost lost in a cloud of flour dust.

"Yes," said Josh, biting into the pie and spraying crumbs of the crust all over the table. "I guess I am."

The back door swung open, and the smell of cabbage wafted in, followed by Josh's dad. Mr. Sanders was a tall man with broad shoulders and a weatherbeaten face. He ducked under the doorframe as he entered.

"Mornin', Josh," he said. "The guanos would like to thank you kindly for their breakfast this morning. They're munching and slurping through it all now." He grinned, barely able to hide his delight. "They also assure me that you'll stop smelling of the stuff within…ooh, a week or two."

Josh grumbled under his breath. He raised an arm and took a deep sniff of his armpit. He definitely smelled bad, although it had been almost a month since his last bath, so he couldn't blame it all on yesterday's vegetable spillage.

"I'm not too sure about that," Josh said. "You could've told me what I was picking up!"

Dad grinned. "Now where'd be the fun in that?"

Mom placed a glass of iguanodon milk in

23

front of Josh and then nodded to the journal he'd put on the table beside him. "You planning on writing something?"

Josh covered the journal protectively. "Uh, no. Yes. Kind of. I'm just doing some…research."

Mom's eyes narrowed. "What kind of research?"

"Nothing big. I mean…nothing interesting."

"I got eight hundred pounds of iguanodon dung and a shovel you could research," said Josh's dad.

The clock on the kitchen wall let out a chime, and a tiny wooden pterodactyl on a spring popped out. Josh swallowed his mouthful of pie, tucked his journal under his arm, and then got to his feet.

"Sorry, Dad." He grinned. "Fun as that sounds, it's time for school!"

Josh stood with Abi and Sam in the line outside the schoolhouse, waiting for the teacher to open the doors. He bounced from foot to foot, clutching his journal to his chest.

"How come you're so full of energy?" Abi asked. "I was up half the night trying to scrub away the stink of rotten greens."

Sam sniffed and then stuck his tongue out. "I don't think it worked."

"That smell's coming off you," Abi pointed out.

Sam lifted the neck of his shirt and sniffed

again. "Oh, yeah," he said, turning a shade of green. "So it is."

"Forget the cabbages," Josh said.

"Not easy standing next to this one," Abi said.

"Look, I've come up with a way of making our life much more exciting," Josh announced. "Seriously, it's amazing. You'll love it."

"You've invented a new type of shoe," Sam guessed.

Josh blinked. "What? No! My plan is—"

"Wait!" said Sam, holding up a hand. "I'll get it." He thought for a moment. "You're going to collect rocks."

"That wouldn't be very exciting," Josh pointed out.

Sam shrugged. "Depends on the rocks."

 26

"Ooh, ooh, I know," said Abi. "You're going to sail across Plesiosaur Lagoon in a barrel? Or…start a dinosaur-walking business."

"Or dress up like T-Bill!" Sam said so loudly that everyone else in the line glanced their way.

"No. None of that," said Josh. "Although I like the barrel idea." He leaned in closer, keeping his voice low. "I…or should I say, *we*, are going to follow in T-Bill's footsteps and catch us a meat eater."

"Catch a tyrannosaurus rex? Are you mad?" Sam whispered.

Josh shook his head. "No, I'm not saying we should catch a T. rex." He shot them a broad smile. "We should go one better. We're going to nab us a giganotosaurus!"

Sam and Abi looked at each other, then burst into laughter.

"Good one," Abi said, tears rolling down her cheeks.

"Catch the biggest and most fearsome meat-eating creature of all time, he says." Sam giggled. "Very funny."

"What's the real plan?" Abi asked.

"That *is* the real plan!" Josh replied, stony-faced. "If we round up a giant, we'll be famous!"

"We'll be lunch," Sam said and gulped.

"Yeah, I think I'd rather swim in cabbage glop," Abi added.

"Come on, guys, we can do this!" Josh urged. Capturing a giant would make a brilliant entry in his dino journal, but it wasn't going to be easy, and he knew he needed his friends to help. Before he could turn on the Sanders charm though, he heard a braying laugh from right behind him.

They turned to find Amos Wilks leering down at them. Amos was a little older than they were and much bigger. His greasy face was layered with pimples, and the wispy beginnings of a moustache sprouted from his top lip.

"Catch a giant?" he said with a snigger. "You couldn't even catch a cold!"

From behind Amos came a high-pitched giggle. The bully's sidekick, Arthur, leaned out from behind the bigger boy's back. "Couldn't catch a cold. Good one."

"Shut up, Arthur!" Amos barked. He stepped

closer to Josh and loomed over him, glaring down. "You might have won the Founders' Day race, but a little dweeb like you would have no chance against a giant."

"I would," Josh said, squaring his shoulders. "I could round one up no problem."

Amos snorted. "Could you now? Well, I got bad news for you. There ain't no giants anywhere near Trihorn."

"Except maybe out by the Scratchclaw Swamps," Arthur said. "I heard a few have been spotted out that way over the years."

Amos shot him an angry glare, and Arthur immediately shrank back. Amos turned back to Josh just as the schoolhouse door opened and the teacher stepped out, ringing the morning bell.

With a final scowl, Amos shouldered past Josh and followed the line into school. Josh began to trudge after them, but Abi and Sam blocked his path.

"So, a giganotosaurus you say? Interesting," said Sam.

"Where do we start?" Abi asked.

Josh's eyes widened. "I thought you weren't interested?"

"We weren't," Abi admitted. "But if Amos Wilks says we can't do it, then we've got no choice but to prove him wrong!"

CHAPTER 3

The end of the school day couldn't come quickly enough for Josh. Each of the day's lessons seemed to drag on and on. Miss Delaney gave the class some homework for the evening, but Josh had already decided he wasn't going to do it. He had other homework of his own.

When the bell finally rang, Josh raced out of the schoolhouse and climbed up onto Charge's

back. The triceratops stomped his feet impatiently. Josh pulled on Charge's reins, guiding him toward Main Street. The dinosaur glanced back in the direction of the ranch, and Josh patted him on the fringe. "Don't worry, boy. We're heading home soon. I just got something to do first."

Charge let out a disappointed snort but followed Josh's lead. They trotted down the street, scaring a pack of aquilops and sending the chicken-size dinos scattering off in all directions.

After squeezing past a baby brontosaurus that was parked near the store, Josh brought Charge to a stop outside the post office. Just before Josh could dismount, there was a high-pitched squawk from overhead.

Pterodactyl, Josh thought as the startled Charge reared up onto his hind legs, his deadly horns stabbing up at the sky. Josh tumbled backward, losing his grip on the reins. He hit the ground hard, then sprang to his feet, already reaching for his lasso. If Charge went chasing after a 'dactyl, he could tear the whole street apart!

Before Josh could let fly with his lasso, a colorful bundle of feathers swished toward him. Josh heard the flutter of wings and saw a flash of deadly claws. He managed to duck, just as a microraptor swooped down and landed on a perch outside the post office. It cocked its head to one side and shot the growling Charge a puzzled look.

Josh got between them and placed a hand

on Charge's nose. "It's OK, buddy. It's just the mail dino!"

Charge panted heavily, his narrowed eyes still fixed on the tiny winged creature. He only looked away when the door to the post office opened and the postmaster emerged. "Afternoon," said the postmaster, unclipping a letter from one of the microraptor's claws.

Josh watched as the postmaster tied a different letter to the microraptor's foot, fed it a snack, then let out a whistle. The birdlike creature lifted into the air, swooped low over Charge's head, and then banked upward toward the sky. Its red, blue, and golden feathers glided smoothly through the air, and its sharp claws glinted in the sun.

Both Josh and Charge watched the little dino shoot upward. When it came to delivering messages on the Lost Plains, there was nothing as fast as the micro mail.

The postmaster kept an eye on the microraptor until it had vanished into the clouds, then turned back toward the door.

"Uh, excuse me," said Josh, stopping him in his tracks.

"Yes? How can I help, Master…Sanders, isn't it?" asked the postmaster, flicking a microraptor feather off his shoulder.

"I was wondering if I might get a look at the Dino Directory?"

The postmaster raised one eyebrow. "Whatever for?"

"It's…for a homework project," Josh said.

The postmaster stroked his moustache thoughtfully. "Well…OK. As long as you're quick and you don't damage it. Those things don't come cheap."

He led Josh through to a small room at the back of the post office. There, sitting in the middle of the room's only table, half-buried under a pile of microraptor feathers, was an enormous guano skin–bound book. The writing on each of its thousands of pages was so tiny that the book came with its own magnifying glass.

Josh pushed the feathers onto the floor, picked up the magnifying glass, and flipped carefully through the book's pages. Each one contained detailed descriptions and diagrams of every type of dinosaur imaginable. All the dinosaurs that roamed the Lost Plains were in there, along with their ancient ancestors who had died off long ago.

After a full ten minutes of searching, Josh found just what he was looking for: the entry on the giganotosaurus. He took his journal from his satchel and set it down beside the Dino Directory. With the magnifying glass in one hand and a pencil in the other, he began to copy out the most important facts.

"Bigger and faster than a T. rex," Josh mumbled as he wrote. "Bad eyesight but attracted by movement and bright colors. Brain the size of a banana."

Josh looked up from the book and frowned. *What's a banana?* he wondered.

With a shrug, he got back to copying. Soon, he had noted down every giganotosaurus fact in the directory. He knew how big it was, how large its footprints were, how much it could eat, and even how much it pooped (which was a lot). He finished the journal entry off with the most accurate drawing he could, then snapped both books shut—if he was going to meet one, he'd be prepared.

Thanking the postmaster, Josh hurried out onto the street. Charge bleated happily when he saw him approaching, but before Josh could start untying the triceratops, his classmate Molly came racing over. Her eyes were

wide, and her breath was coming in big, shaky gasps.

"What's wrong?" asked Josh. "What happened?"

"You won't believe what I just heard on the news grapevine!" Molly said.

"What is it?" asked Josh.

Molly shook her head. "No point telling you," she said. "You won't believe it!"

"Believe *what*?"

"Can't explain. You gotta see for yourself," she said. "Saddle up, quick."

Josh swung himself up into Charge's saddle, then slid forward as Molly clambered up behind him. "Where are we going?" he asked.

"Cross the river, near the edge of the Lost Plains," Molly said. "And be quick about it!"

With a shouted "Yah!" Josh urged Charge into action. The triceratops roared in triumph, finally free to run. His feet churned up the ground as they raced toward the Lost Plains.

"There!" Molly cried when they crossed the reinforced bridge that stretched across the narrow river. A small group of townsfolk had gathered and were scratching their heads as they stared down at something on the ground.

Josh jumped down before Charge had fully stopped moving. He and Molly hurried through the crowd until they saw what everyone was staring at. It was a shape, clearly marked out on the dry ground.

It took a moment until Josh realized what he was looking at. It was a footprint. A big one.

No, not big—*giant*... And it could have come from only one dino.

CHAPTER 4

The night following the giganotosaurus footprint discovery, Josh barely slept a wink. He spent an hour or more writing about the finding in his dino journal, then lay in bed, tossing and turning until the sun came up. By the time he joined Sam and Abi on the plod to school, he was bouncing in the saddle with excitement.

"So I've been thinking," he babbled, steering

Charge around a bend in the track. "If the giant footprint was out over the river, then it had to have come from out west. Right?"

Abi shrugged. "Suppose."

"Are we sure it was definitely a giant print though?" Sam asked.

"Definitely! You should have seen it. I could have laid down in it with my arms above my head and still not have touched the toes. It was a giant, all right," Josh insisted. "So let's just say it came from out west. What else is out west?"

"The sunset?" Sam asked.

"What? No!"

"It is," Sam said. "The sun rises in the east and sets in the west. That's just a fact."

"He's right," agreed Abi, digging her heels into her gallimimus's side to spur it over a mound in the road. "The sun definitely sets in the west."

"Yes, but the giganotosaurus didn't come from the sunset, did it?" Josh said.

"So where did it come from?" Sam asked.

"From the Scratchclaw Swamps!" Josh said triumphantly. "Arthur said there were giants spotted out that way before."

Abi looked doubtful. "I wouldn't trust Arthur if he told me the sky was blue."

"Neither would I, but you saw how Amos reacted, right? He was angry that Arthur told us about the swamp," said Josh. "Because he knows it's true."

"I suppose…it could be right," Sam admitted.

"Maybe," Abi said and then groaned. "You're going to make us check it out after school, aren't you?"

Josh shook his head. "No, of course not," he said. He tugged on Charge's reins, steering the triceratops off to the left. "I'm going to make us check it out *before* school!"

Josh, Sam, and Abi stood on a narrow ridge, peering down into a pit of gloopy green goo. Bubbles rose up on its surface, releasing clouds of stinky gas when they popped. It reminded Josh of the sloppy cabbage buckets but on a much bigger—and smellier—scale.

Charge and the other dinos were tied up a safe distance from the edge of the swamp. The path had vanished a couple of miles back, and the rocky terrain had gradually become more and more difficult for the huge beasts to cross. Dark, towering boulders now stood all around the children, casting cold shadows across the ground. Crumbling ledges jutted out above the swamps like diving boards. No one would be fool enough to dive into the swamp though.

In fact, it was rare for anyone to pay a visit to the Scratchclaw Swamps. Those who ventured into the area usually did so by accident and often didn't come back out. The swamps were the final resting place of many a careless traveler—and even more careless dinos.

Bleached white bones jutted out from beneath the bubbling surface of the nearest swampy pool. Josh recognized it as a triceratops skeleton. The poor dino must have wandered too close to the bogs and been unable to escape their powerful suction. Josh glanced back over his shoulder, hoping he'd tied Charge's reins good and tight.

 54

"I can't see any giants," Sam said, his voice muffled by the neckerchief he'd tied over his nose to block out the smell.

Josh looked around. "Maybe it's hiding."

Abi snorted. "Hiding? It's fifty times taller than us! Where would it hide?"

"Well, it's probably only about ten times taller," Josh mumbled. "Depending on age, how it's standing, and…" He sighed. "OK, you're right. It's probably not hiding."

"Oh well, it was worth a try," Sam chirped. "Off to school we go!"

"Wait," Josh pleaded. "We have to look *properly*. Just in case."

Sam couldn't hide his sarcasm. "Yes. Let's take a little more time to look for the deadliest dinosaur in existence," he said. "I'd *hate* for us to miss it…"

The three friends split up to cover more ground. Josh crept along a narrow ledge overhanging a slime-coated pool. Choking swamp gas hung in a hazy cloud above it. Josh held his breath as he hurried across.

He didn't dare go too fast though. The gas hung in the air like a thick fog, making it difficult to see. Shapes seemed to lunge out of the mist, as if the ghosts of all those who'd been lost here were trying to drag Josh down with them.

Once he'd made it across the ledge, Josh searched for *anything* that might suggest a giant was nearby. Another footprint would do. He'd even be happy if he stumbled upon a massive mound of steaming dino dung. At least then he'd know that he had a chance of finding an actual giganotosaurus.

No matter which way he looked though, there was nothing. No footprints. No dung. No dinosaur. Josh sighed. "This is a waste of time," he muttered.

Suddenly, he heard a cry from Sam. "Guys! Come here! Quick!"

Doubling back, Josh scurried across the ledge and scrambled up an incline, following Sam's voice. Abi was already there when Josh reached the jagged outcrop of rock where Sam was kneeling.

"What is it? Did you see a giant?" Josh asked.

Sam shook his head. "Do you think I'd still

be hanging around here if I did? I'd be halfway back to Trihorn by now."

Josh couldn't help but be disappointed. "Well, why did you shout at us?"

Sam pointed down into the swamp below. "Look."

Cautiously, Josh and Abi approached the edge and followed Sam's finger. Abi let out a low whistle, and Josh felt his heart begin to thump like a drum inside his chest. There, half-buried in the trunk of a fallen tree, was the biggest tooth any of them had ever seen.

"That's a giant's tooth," Josh whispered.

"Oh, goody," Sam said. "I was hoping you'd say that." He glanced around nervously. "We should probably get going."

Sam stood just as the rock ledge beneath them gave a shudder. The friends froze, wide-eyed in panic.

"What was that?" Abi asked.

Josh spun, scanning the area around them.

"I think it might be a giant," he croaked, his voice suddenly dry.

The ground shook again, but this time, the rumble was joined by a gloopy *schlurp*. A spray of swamp water lapped against the edge of the outcrop.

Sam let out a laugh of relief. "No, it isn't! It's just the swamp bubbling," he said. "It's probably just a geyser or something."

The smile quickly fell from his face. "Wait," Sam said and frowned. "Geyser?"

With a *whoosh*, a tower of stinking swamp glop erupted upward right beside them. Wads of thick green goo splattered the friends from head to toe. Josh closed his eyes to shield them from the spray.

A moment later, he scooped away the slime and forced his eyes open. Abi stood before him, wiping the swamp sludge from her own face.

But Sam was nowhere to be seen!

CHAPTER 5

Josh dived for the edge just in time to see Sam hit the swamp with a *splat*. Sam thrashed frantically in the sludge, gasping and spluttering as he struggled to stay afloat.

"Swim, Sam!" Abi yelled.

"Trying…my…best!" Sam replied.

"He won't be able to tread swamp for long," Josh realized. "We have to help him."

"Throw him your lasso!" Abi cried.

Josh grabbed for the rope slung at his waist. "Of course!" he yelled. With a flick of his wrist, he tossed the lasso down toward Sam. It hit the swamp beside him and immediately sank out of sight.

"You were meant to keep hold of one end!" Abi cried.

Josh gulped. "Oh. Yeah. That makes more sense."

Sam struggled against the pull of the swamp slime. They'd already seen it was powerful enough to drag down a triceratops, and Sam's strokes were growing slower.

"What now?" Abi asked.

Josh lay on the rock and stretched down,

trying to reach Sam. It was no use though. No matter how far he stretched, he couldn't get close enough to grab him.

"Hold my ankles," he said, glancing back at Abi.

Abi quickly caught hold of Josh's legs. Gritting her teeth, she lowered him down toward the thrashing Sam.

"Stay still!" Josh urged as he tried to catch Sam's wrist.

"I can't!" Sam said. The rest of his reply came out as a stream of bubbles as his head dipped below the surface.

With a frantic grab, Josh caught hold of Sam's wrist. "Pull us up, Abi!" he called, but the only reply was a groan of effort. "Hurry!"

"You're too heavy," Abi said with a wheeze. "I can't hold on!"

Josh's stomach lurched as Abi lost her footing. She stumbled toward the edge, still holding Josh's ankles. They were going to fall…

Yoink! Something hooked through her belt, stopping her.

"Charge!" she yelled as the burly triceratops snorted his arrival.

Josh looked back to see Charge's giant, central horn holding his friend upright in the air.

"Good one, boy!" he cheered. "Now pull!"

Charge scuffed the ground and motored backward. Abi held on to Josh, and Josh held on to Sam, who was eventually yanked from the swamp with a noisy *shlurrrpp*. The force of Charge's pull sent them collapsing onto the side of the ledge, all three of them panting, wheezing, and dripping with stinky green slime. Josh covered his head with his hands as Charge tried to lick the glop off him.

"Urgh, Charge. Thanks, but that's enough!" he said with a laugh. "Swamp slime and dino slobber are not a good mix!"

They lay there for a moment, getting their breath back. "Well," Sam said at last, "I think I've had enough giant hunting for one day. One lifetime, actually."

"What? But we can't give up now," Josh protested.

"Sam's right," said Abi. She groaned and

sat up. "If there was a giant here, it's long gone. And we should be too, or we'll be late for school."

Josh tried to argue, but Sam and Abi had made their minds up. Suddenly, he found himself riding to school, smelly, soggy, and sad. They arrived after class had started, and when they squelched through the door, a roar of laughter from their classmates met them. Even the teacher, who rarely cracked a smile, had to hide her grin behind her hand as she looked them up and down.

"What happened to you three?" Amos asked from the back of the class. "Been eating break-fast with the iguanodons again?"

"Ha-ha! Very good!" Arthur said with a giggle

before Amos shot him a stern look. "Shutting up now, sir," the smaller boy whimpered.

"If you must know, we were out at the Scratchclaw Swamps," Josh said. "Hunting down a giant."

Amos snorted. "What happened? Did it blow its nose on you?"

"A giant?" asked Miss Delaney, who had now composed herself. "As in a giganotosaurus? That sounds very dangerous."

"Don't worry. We didn't find one," said Sam, which made Amos snort out another laugh.

"But we almost did," protested Josh.

"Did you almost find the tooth fairy while you were at it?" Amos cackled.

The rest of the class joined in, and Josh felt

his cheeks sting red. His fists clenched, and he stamped his foot on the floor.

"There *is* a giant out there, and I can prove it!" he snapped.

Amos raised an eyebrow. "Oh yeah? How?"

"Because we'll catch it, that's how! Before school tomorrow, out at Scratchclaw," Josh said. "We're going to catch us a giganotosaurus!"

The class erupted into laughter once

more. Abi and Sam both shot Josh a worried look. "What did you say that for?" Abi asked.

"They'll all laugh at us when we don't catch one," Sam said.

"They're laughing at us now," Josh pointed out. "Besides, I know how we're going to do it."

Abi and Sam both frowned. "How?" Abi asked.

Josh smiled. "If we can't go out and find a giant, then we'll just have to make a giant come to us!"

After school—and baths—Josh, Sam, and Abi gathered in Josh's barn. Josh had decided they

Attach ropes to the giant and let a team of pterodactyls carry them away

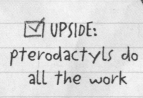 ☑ UPSIDE: pterodactyls do all the work

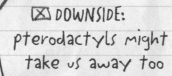 ☒ DOWNSIDE: pterodactyls might take us away too

Create mousetrap the size of a house

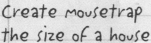

☑ UPSIDE: will make quick work of the giant

 ☒ DOWNSIDE: we'll need a small mountain of cheese

were going to build the world's first giganoto-saurus trap. The only problem was, they had absolutely no idea how to start.

"What if we dug a big hole?" suggested Sam.

Josh rubbed his chin. "How big?"

"Giganotosaurus size," Sam said.

Josh looked at the drawing of the giant in his journal and tried to imagine how long it would take to dig a hole that size. Weeks, probably. Maybe months.

"No time for that," he said. He looked hope-fully at Abi. "Any other suggestions?"

"A catapult?"

Josh leaned forward. This sounded more like it. "What sort of catapult?"

Abi shrugged. "Dunno."

"Well, what would it do?" Josh asked.

Abi shrugged again. "Dunno. I hadn't really thought it through," she admitted. "It sounded cool though."

Josh paced back and forth as he tried to think. "We need something simple. Something that's been tried and tested."

"I don't think anyone's tried building a giant trap before," Sam pointed out.

Josh stopped. His eyes went wide. "Sam, you're a genius!"

"I am?" Sam frowned. "I mean...yes. Yes, I am." He smiled weakly. "Which part was genius, exactly?"

"To trap a giant, we need a giant trap."

Abi and Sam exchanged a glance. "Erm, yes.

That's what we've been trying to come up with," Abi said.

Josh rummaged in an old wooden chest in the corner of the barn and pulled out a length of rope. "No, I don't mean a giant trap. I mean a *giant trap*."

Abi blinked. "Well, that makes things much clearer."

Josh tossed the rope over one of the barn's wooden rafters and began looping the ends together. "You're not getting it," he said with a sigh. "I don't mean a giant trap. I mean a trap which we've made giant size."

He took one end of the looped-up rope and tied it around the wooden chest. With a heave, he hauled on the rope, raising the chest into the air. "Like a snare!" he said, nodding in the direction of the circle of rope he'd left on the barn's wooden floor.

Abi and Sam slowly approached the rope loop and peered down at it.

"Obviously, we'd need a bigger rope," Josh said.

His friends looked doubtful. "It'll never work," Abi said. She stepped into the loop. "There's no way this thing will—waaaaaah!"

She yelled in fright as the loop tightened around her legs. Josh released his grip on the rope, and the chest fell, jerking Abi into the air. She scowled as she swung upside down on the rope. Josh and Sam both doubled over as they began to laugh.

"Sorry, Abi," Josh said as he giggled. "You were saying?"

"T a-da!"

Josh and Dad both stared at the plate Mom had set in the middle of the table. On it was heaped a great big mound of mashed potatoes. But it was like no mashed potatoes either of them had ever seen.

Pieces of broccoli sprouted from the top like a forest of tiny trees. A little log cabin had been built from a few iguanodon sausages, and the whole thing was swimming in a sea of thick, brown gravy.

"What in the name of all that is scaly is that?" asked Dad, eyeing the meal suspiciously.

"It's dinner," Mom said. "I read in a book that it's important for a meal to be a feast for the eyes as well as for the belly."

"You could've just made a pie," said Dad.

"I did." Mom beamed. She used a spoon to

scoop aside a clump of the soggy potatoes, revealing a piecrust lurking beneath. "It's mini ranch pie. There's the ranch," she said, pointing to the sausage cabin. "There's the forest, and that there's the river."

"It's brown," said Josh.

"Well, so is the river half the time," said Mom defensively. "Besides, you try finding blue gravy."

Dad puffed out his cheeks. "It's..."

"A feast for the eyes," said Mom, shooting him a dangerous look. "That's what you were going to say, wasn't it?"

Dad nodded quickly. "Yes, ma'am. It's a feast for the eyes." He scooped a lump of the mash onto his plate and plucked out a few of the trees.

Mom smiled approvingly and took her seat. "It's important for a meal to look attractive. You've got to make it enticing."

Josh started to scoop the mash onto his own plate as Mom's words echoed in his head. "Make it enticing," he mumbled.

Of course! He couldn't expect the giant to just wander up to the snare. He had to find a way of luring it. The trap had to be…

"A feast for the eyes!" he said.

He looked up and realized Mom and Dad were both watching him closely.

"Uh…you got enough potato there, Josh?" Mom asked.

Josh glanced down at his plate. He'd scooped almost all the gravy-soaked mash into his own dish. He smiled awkwardly. "Uh…you can never have too much potato," he said.

After his mound of mash, Josh tried to sneak away, but Dad had other ideas. The iguanodon pens needed clearing out, and Josh hadn't taken his turn in days. Armed with a shovel and a bundle of sacks, Josh trudged out to the pens. The smell that hung in the air almost choked him as he approached, but all the while, he was wondering about the giant trap.

What can I use to lure the giganotosaurus? he wondered. The Dino Directory had said the big dinosaur's favorite snack was microraptors, but he couldn't exactly pluck one of those out of the sky.

With a *squelch*, Josh trod in a blob of

iguanodon poo. It squidged up around his boot and almost stuck him to the floor when he tried to pull free. "Man, this stuff's sticky," he muttered.

Josh stared at the bottom of his boot. "Sticky," he whispered. His mind raced. "Microraptors."

And suddenly, Josh knew exactly what to do.

Next morning, Josh slid down from Charge's back and tied him securely to a tree beside Abi's and Sam's dinos. He unhooked the two sacks he'd brought with him. One of them, he held on to easily, while the other dropped to the ground with a heavy thud.

Pausing to give Charge a pat, Josh hurried up the rocky track leading to the start of the Scratchclaw Swamps, carrying one of the sacks and dragging the other behind him.

He'd taught his friends how to set the snare, and they'd just finished hooking the rope over the branch of a tall pine tree that stood at the swamp's edge. Josh made sure to avoid stepping in the loop so he didn't face the same fate as Abi had back at the barn.

"The trap's all set," Sam announced.

Josh shook his head. "Not yet it isn't," he said.

"How come?" Abi asked. "We did it just like you showed us."

Josh dropped the sacks on the ground. "I forgot one thing. Bait."

Sam raised an eyebrow. "Bait?"

"What do giants like to eat?" Josh asked, opening the lighter of the two sacks.

"Children?" Sam gulped.

"Everything?" said Abi.

"Well, yes," Josh admitted. "But there's something they like most of all."

He pulled out a bundle of colorful feathers he'd collected from the post office floor on the way to the swamps. "Microraptors."

Josh's friends looked at the feathers. They looked at Josh. "I don't get it," they both said at once.

"We'll stick these feathers on, do a bit of squawking and flapping, and make the giant think we're microraptors," Josh said.

"Great!" yelled Sam. "Then it can eat us alive!"

"No, then we'll lure it to the snare and catch it," said Josh. "It's a genius plan."

Abi crossed her arms. "OK, genius, how exactly are we supposed to stick feathers to ourselves?"

Josh opened the second sack. A cloud of flies flew out, followed by a waft of stinky air. Sam and Abi both stepped back, their eyes widening in horror. Josh reached into the bag and scooped out a handful of six-month-old guano manure. He slapped it onto the side of his face with a *splat*, then pressed some feathers into it.

"Tell me you're not serious," Abi said with a groan.

"Deadly serious," Josh said. "Now grab some dino dung and feather up. That giant could be here any minute!"

CHAPTER

7

osh, Sam, and Abi danced in a circle, flapping their arms and squawking at the top of their lungs. Dollops of dino manure dribbled off them and splattered on the dusty ground. Dozens of brightly colored feathers were squished into the sticky mixture, and if they flapped and screeched enough, they could almost pass for very large microraptors. Josh called it the dino dance and was hollering as loud as he could.

"This is ridiculous," Sam protested.

"We look like crazy people!" Abi added.

"It's OK," Josh assured his friends as he did a particularly spectacular dino dance move. "It'll be worth it when we catch the giant!"

"You owe us big-time for this," Abi said with a growl.

Aaa-tchoo! Sam sneezed, blowing a flurry of feathers off his face. "I think I might be allergic to microraptors," he said as he sniffed.

Suddenly, there was a sound from behind them. The three friends turned, bracing themselves to find a giganotosaurus rearing upward. Instead, they saw something far worse.

Amos's laugh echoed all around the swamp. He and Arthur pointed and cackled at the sight of Josh, Abi, and Sam coated in feathers and dino dung. Behind the bullies, Molly scrambled up the track and gasped in surprise.

"Oh boy," Amos said. "This is better than I could've dreamed of! Look at them! What do they look like?"

"Microraptors?" Arthur suggested.

"*Idiots*, Arthur," Amos snapped. "They look like idiots."

"Yeah! That's what I meant," Arthur said and sneered. "They look like idiots!"

Abi and Sam blushed and quickly scraped the sticky feather mixture off their faces.

Molly had her notebook out and was frantically taking notes. "Wow, this is going to make a great story for the newspaper," she said, which only made Amos laugh even louder.

"You won't be laughing when we catch the giant," Josh said.

Amos stepped closer, then waved his hand in front of his face and stepped back again. "Wow, you stink," he said. "And there's no way you're going to catch a giant."

Josh clenched his fists. "Yes, we are!"

"There is no giant!" Amos said, grinning triumphantly. "Don't you get it? We set you up!"

Josh frowned. "Wh-what are you talking about?"

"All that talk about the swamps…the big footprint that so *conveniently* turned up right outside of town… That was me!" Amos crowed. "All me!"

"Well, *us*," Arthur added, but Amos shot him a mean look. "Him," Arthur whimpered. "It was him."

"N-no," said Josh, shaking his head. He couldn't believe it. He wouldn't. "No, there is a giant out here, and we're going to catch it!"

Molly scribbled frantically. "This is good stuff. Keep going," she urged.

93

"Oh, grow up, Sanders," Amos barked. "Hardly anyone's seen a giant up close. Do you honestly think one just happened to show up the day we heard you talking about catching one outside school? I set you up because I knew you'd end up making a fool of yourself—just like T-Bill." He looked the dung-coated trio up and down. "But wow, you've really taken it to a new level this time."

Josh felt his cheeks burning up. He looked at his manure-splattered friends, plucking their feathers off. He looked down at himself and realized that Amos was right. He did look ridiculous.

"So you did all of it?" he asked, the words coming out as a hiss.

"Yep!" said Amos proudly.

"The tooth too?" Josh asked.

Amos and Arthur looked at one another. "What tooth?" Amos asked.

"The giant tooth," Josh said. "The one we found stuck into the tree trunk."

Amos shrugged. "I don't know what you're talking about."

Boom!

The ground beneath the children trembled, making Molly's pencil slip across her page. "What was that?" she asked, just as the rock beneath them shook once more.

Slowly, Josh turned and peered at the closest swampy pool. The surface rippled as the ground rumbled again.

A shadow fell across the children. Josh, Sam, Abi, Amos, Arthur, and Molly all craned their necks to look up. A monster glared down at them.

A monster with one missing tooth.

Josh turned to Amos, his throat suddenly dry. "T-told you," he said.

And that was when the screaming started.

CHAPTER 8

Eeeeeeeearghhhh!"

Arthur's shriek was so high-pitched, it could have shattered glass. He ran in circles, pointing frantically up at the giganotosaurus, which was now thundering toward them.

"What do we do?" Amos babbled. "What do we do?"

"Flap!" Josh said, waving his arms around. "Flap and squawk! Lead it to the snare!"

All the children began to flap and screech like microraptors, trying to draw the giant toward the trap.

"It's w-working," said Sam. "Here it comes!"

Sure enough, the giant was closing in fast. Josh had to lean back to see the entirety of the enormous creature. He'd known it'd be big, but it was far larger than he'd been prepared for.

Its broad head seemed to scrape the clouds. Its huge jaws looked like they could have swallowed Charge whole and still left room for dessert. He stood staring at it, rooted to the spot, until Abi dragged him out of the great beast's path.

"Move!" she urged, hauling Josh to safety.

The children scattered just as the giant

stepped on the snare. The rope went tight around one of the dinosaur's hind legs. Josh began to cheer, but it quickly turned into a groan when the giant's next step tore the tree right out of the ground.

"Oh, great trap, Josh!" Sam yelped. "Brilliant design!"

"I knew we should've used a catapult," Abi muttered.

"We're all going to die!" squealed Arthur.

"Sh!" Josh hissed, silencing everyone.

The only sound was the scratching of Molly's pencil. Abi nudged her with an elbow.

"Sorry," Molly whispered. "But this is good stuff."

"Nobody move," said Josh. The giganotosaurus

was right in front of them, its enormous head swinging slowly left and right. "It has terrible eyesight. It can only see bright colors."

"We're covered in bright colors," Sam squeaked.

"We'll be OK if we all stand completely still," Josh whispered. "It won't notice us. Probably."

"Probably?" Abi asked.

The ground shook again as the giant took a step closer. It lowered its head, sniffing the air. The beast's skull was so big, it blocked out most of the sky. Josh and the others held their breath as nostrils larger than their heads snuffled and snorted closer.

The giant's neck stretched forward until the dino's snout was almost touching Josh. He was sure the beast would hear the thudding of his heartbeat and had to fight every urge to turn and run.

With a deep sniff, the giant inhaled half a dozen of the feathers Josh had stuck to himself. It tilted its head to the side, its gums drawing up in what looked like a snarl but was in fact—

Aaa-tchoo!

The giant sneezed, spraying the group with

103

stringy strands of sticky snot and slobber. Josh, Abi, Sam, and Molly stood their ground, but it was all too much for cowardly Amos and Arthur.

"Let's get out of here!" Amos shrieked. He and Arthur stumbled, half-blinded by globs of green snot, and ran screaming back in the direction of town.

"Amos, don't!" Josh yelled. "We have to stay still."

Too late! With a deafening roar, the giant turned. Josh, Abi, Sam, and Molly threw themselves to the ground to avoid being swatted by its tail. When they got back to their feet, the giant was already chasing after Amos and Arthur and gaining fast.

Josh wasn't a big fan of Amos and Arthur, but

he knew if he didn't do something, the bullies would be the giant's next snack. Spotting a length of the snare rope on the ground, he quickly snatched it up and raced after the giant, snapping the rope out in front of him like his lasso.

"Hey! Ugly! Down here!" he cried. The rope whipped the end of the giant's tail. Josh skidded to a stop as the flesh eater spun around to face him, letting out a furious roar. "Um, OK. This was a bad idea," he whimpered.

The giganotosaurus lunged, its teeth snapping hungrily. Josh dived to safety just in time and rolled to his feet. He looked around, searching for an escape route but instead finding something even better.

Waving his arms, Josh began to run. "This way!" he yelled. "Follow me, you big brute!"

Abi, Sam, and Molly ducked for cover as Josh raced past. He could feel the breath of the giant on his back as he powered toward the edge of a rocky outcrop. His heart pounded. His stomach went tight. *This is gonna be close!* he thought.

As Josh reached the edge, he threw himself sideways and rolled to a clumsy stop on the ground. The giant tried to turn, but it was going too fast. It skidded straight toward the edge…

"Please fall in, please fall in, please fall in," Josh whispered as he watched the giant fight to stay upright. It was teetering on the edge but was using its tail to keep itself balanced.

Suddenly, the ground began to shake again,

much faster than before. Josh felt a wind whistle past him and heard a very familiar snort. Charge lowered his head and hit the giant like a battering ram. The giant meat eater roared in anger as it stumbled forward, then let out a panicked yelp as it tumbled over the edge and into the swamp below.

A spray of stinking swamp water was thrown high into the air over Josh's head. He followed its flight and couldn't help but laugh when he realized where it was going to land.

Amos and Arthur looked up just in time to be covered in the smelly sludge. It knocked them to the ground, plastering them against the rocks.

A sandpaper-like tongue licked Josh's face,

and for once, he didn't try to fight it off. "Charge, am I glad to see you!" he cheered, throwing his arms around his dino's snout and hugging him tightly.

Abi, Sam, and Molly raced over to Josh's side, and all took turns patting Charge and

exchanging happy high fives. The friends gingerly took a look over the edge of the outcrop. Aside from a few ripples in the swamp water below, the giant was nowhere to be seen.

"How did you know it would follow you?" Sam asked.

"They're not very clever," Josh explained. "Their brains are the size of a banana."

Abi frowned. "What's a banana?"

"I have no idea," Josh admitted. "But I'm guessing it's not very big."

"One thing I do know," began Molly. She held up her notebook. "This time tomorrow, you're gonna be front-page news! Terrordactyl Bill couldn't have done it better himself!"

Josh grinned from ear to ear. He had battled

a giganotosaurus, saved his friends, and proved Amos wrong. Yep, days didn't come much better than that.

"Oh no, I've just remembered something," Sam said with a gasp. "We're late for school!"

They all turned and raced for their dinos as quickly as they could. Josh swung up into Charge's saddle and steered his trusty steed down the slope. Facing off against an angry giganotosaurus was one thing, but facing off against an angry Miss Delaney? Even T-Bill would think twice about that.

Josh and Charge galloped past Amos and Arthur as they tried to get to their feet on the slippery ground. "Phew," Josh said, waving his hand in front of his face. "You guys stink."

And with that, Josh and Charge sped toward Trihorn settlement—and toward their next big adventure.

LOCAL BOY SWAMPS GIANT!

dino sinks without a trace
in Scratchclaw Swamps. The only

Trihorn saved from destruction!

CHAPTER 1

Josh Sanders and his best friends, Sam and Abi, held their breath as an iguanodon loudly *parped* a cloud of toxic gas in front of them. They were trotting along on their dinosaurs—Sam and Abi both riding their trusty gallimimuses, while Josh rocked in the saddle of Charge, his triceratops.

Overhead, the afternoon sun blazed down. Before them, a thousand iguanodons plodded their way across a vast, barren plain, headed for the snow-topped Wandering Mountains a few miles ahead.

Once a year, Josh and his friends would join half the adults in Trihorn settlement on the iguanodon drive out to Scaly Point. A rancher could make a lot of money selling guanos at Scaly Point, and although it meant a three-week round trip, Josh loved every minute of it.

Well, *most* minutes of it. Iguanodons were smelly beasts at the best of times, and being stuck behind a thousand of them sure made his eyes water.

"So today is day seven, right?" asked Abi, trotting along on Josh's left.

The Journey So Far:

DAY 1: Head out with the herd.

DAY 2: Splodge through the Scratchclaw Swamps. Lose a shoe in the quicksand.

DAY 3: Sneak through Cold Fear Forest. Almost get eaten by a dragonfly the size of my head.

DAY 4: Survive stampeding iguanodons.

DAY 5: Survive iguanodon stink cloud.

DAY 6: Arrive at the staging post to gather vital supplies. Get new shoe.

"Uh, I think so," Josh replied, flicking through his notebook to make sure.

"Correct," said Sam over on Josh's right. "By the end of today, we will officially be one-third of the way through the journey."

"Only a week until we reach Scaly Point," said Josh.

"Only?" Abi groaned. "My saddle sores have saddle sores. I reckon that bed back at the staging post was made of razor wire and rocks."

"True," Sam said and nodded. "The beds were lousy, but there was one thing the staging post was good for…" He reached into his overflowing saddlebags and pulled out a colorful paper bag. "Candy!"

Josh and Abi both laughed.

"That's not all candy in there, is it?" asked Josh.

"Indeed it is," said Sam. "You can never have too much!"

"I think the dentist might disagree with you," said Abi.

"Yes, but he's not here," Sam replied. "Try this stuff—it's amazing!"

He reached across and poured some shimmering yellow powder from the bag into Josh's hand. Josh passed some across to Abi, and they both tipped the powder into their mouths at the same time. At first, nothing happened. The powder tasted OK, but it was nothing special. Josh was about to say as much when he felt a tingling on his tongue.

"What the—" he began. But before he finished, the powder fizzed against his gums. His eyes went wide. His lips went tight. He gasped, and his face twisted up as an explosion of sourness went *pop-pop-pop* inside his mouth. It tasted partly like lemon, partly like lime, and partly like the powder Josh's mom used to do the laundry, and it jumped around inside his mouth like a diplodocus playing hopscotch.

Josh glanced at Abi,

whose face was also twisted up. They both opened their mouths at the same time, and lots of fizzing yellow foam dribbled down their chins.

"What is that stuff?" Abi asked as she gasped.

"It's called Tasty TNT popping candy!" He laughed as he tucked the bag back into his saddle. "Good, isn't it?"

"Great," Josh said with a wheeze. "It nearly blew my head off!"

There was a thunder of dino feet beside them, and Josh's dad rode up. He took one look at Abi and Josh and asked, "Something happen to your face?"

"Tasty TNT," Josh said. "Don't ask."

Dad nodded and tipped his hat back. "Fair enough. There's a narrow pass through the mountains up ahead. Reckon I'll go help lead from the front and try to squeeze the guanos through. You OK hanging back here to watch for stragglers?"

Josh touched the brim of his hat. "Sure thing, Dad."

"Attaboy," Dad said, leaning across and patting his son on the shoulder. "Knew I could count on you three. Yah!"

He kicked with his heels, and his dinosaur sprang forward. Josh watched him weave and dodge through the iguanodon herd until he was lost in the clouds of dust and sand churned up by the animals' heavy feet.

Sam sighed. "We couldn't be up front. We had to be back here at the smelly end."

As if on cue, an iguanodon right in front of him raised a back leg.

"Oh, hey, I picked up something at the staging post store too," said Abi, rummaging in her saddle bag.

"It's not more Tasty TNT, is it?" Josh asked.

Abi pulled out a bundle of paper and passed it over. "It's the *Daily Diplodocus*," she explained. "Got news about T-Bill."

Josh took the newspaper eagerly. Terrordactyl Bill was his all-time hero and the greatest dino wrangler the world had ever seen. His exploits were legendary, and Josh tried to model himself on T-Bill in every way, right down to his hat.

"T-Bill stopped a T. rex from trampling a town using just a tiny stick of dynamite!" he read. "Says here the explosion discombobu-lated the T. rex, which then ran away, leaving the town completely safe. Wow!"

He was about to carry on when the paper was snatched from his hands. Josh looked up into the greasy, grinning face of his archenemy.

"Amos," he spat. "Give that back!"

Amos Wilks sneered as he weaved his club-tailed ankylosaurus out of Josh's reach. "Says here the explosion took out half of the town's saloon," Amos read. "So much for leaving it safe!"

"Yeah," sniggered Amos's weasel-faced side-kick, Arthur, who was scurrying along on his own gallimimus. "So much for leaving it safe!"

"Shut up, Arthur," Amos snapped.

"Shutting up," said Arthur meekly.

"What do you know, Amos?" Josh asked, making another grab for the newspaper.

"I know plenty," Amos told him. "Fact is, I'm a better dino wrangler than T-Bill ever was. I could wrestle a T. rex to a standstill with my bare hands."

"With your bad breath, maybe," Abi muttered.

"I still don't get why you're here," Josh said. "You don't know anything about herding guanos."

"Maybe I just wanted to keep you company," said Amos. He tore the newspaper in half and let the wind carry it off. "And let you see what a *real* hero looks like."

"You?" Josh snorted. "You must be joking!"

"Guys?" said Sam.

"I'm stronger and braver than that stupid T-Bill any day!"

Josh growled. "You take that back."

"Guys, look!" Sam shouted. He pointed to where the guano herd had started to pull ahead. They were already at the narrow mountain pass—the only safe track leading through the Wandering Mountains. "We're falling behind."

"Last one there's a brontosaurus butt," Amos cried, kicking his ankylosaurus hard and sending it racing across the plain. Josh and the others hurried after him, and the booming of all five sets of dino feet shook the ground around them.

But that wasn't all that was shaking, Josh

realized as they reached the edge of the mountain pass. Tiny pebbles were rolling and clattering down the hill beside him. A larger rock bounced off the ground with a *crack*.

Suddenly, there was a rumbling from up high—loud enough to be heard even over the footsteps and the low calls of the entire guano herd. Josh and the others rocked violently in their saddles as the ground beneath them shook.

Abi let out a sharp gasp, then pointed upward. A torrent of rocks and stones were tumbling and rolling down the mountainside toward them.

"Avalanche!" she cried.

"Well, technically, it's a landslide," Sam began.

But before Abi had a chance to call him a smarty pants, the rumbling continued, dust filled the air, and a whole slab of mountain came crashing toward them.

ABOUT THE AUTHOR

Ever since he was a little boy, Will Dare has been mad about T. rexes and velociraptors. He always wondered what it would be like to live in a world where they were still alive. Now, grown up, he has put pen to paper and imagined just that world. Will lives in rural America with his wife and his best pal, Charge (a dog, not a triceratops).